123 GULLS

A Counting Book by Beth Rand

ISLANDPORT PRESS

Text and illustrations © 2018 by Beth Rand

Published by Islandport Press
P.O. Box 10
Yarmouth, Maine 04096
books@islandportpress.com
www.islandportpress.com

ISBN: 978-1-944762-52-0
Library of Congress Control Number: 2018940793
Printed in USA

For my favorite trio—Matt, Lindsay, and Natalie. Love you all!

Ten mittens in bright hues

9

Nine hats in
reds and blues

Eight scarves to fight the freeze

Seven shells in the breeze

Six sunglasses to shield the eyes

 Five mugs of cocoa
under blue skies

4

Four snowshoes making tracks

Three carrots packed as snacks

2 Two branches
from a tree

1

One snowman
by the sea

10

Ten snowballs in a fight

Fifty snowflakes soft and white

100

One hundred stars
twinkling bright

1

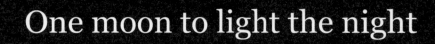
One moon to light the night

About the Author

Photo by Jeff Rand

Beth Rand is a self-taught illustrator who has published her own line of greeting cards and a poster calendar featuring Maine imagery. *123 Gulls* is a companion to *ABC Gulls,* which came out in 2017.

Born in Pittsburgh, Pennsylvania, having a Navy dentist for a dad meant that Rand had an itinerant childhood, moving from Maryland to Rhode Island to South Carolina and even Sicily. Since graduating from the University of Maine, she has made Maine her home. For twenty years, she and her husband lived in Cape Elizabeth, where they successfully raised three children to adulthood. Then they hopped on the ferry to Peaks Island, and never looked back. Rand now lives on the island with her husband and dog, in a home surrounded by seagulls, sunshine, and salt air. When foul weather keeps her inside, illustration becomes the focus.

My favorite winter activity is a walk along the shore with my dog, Charlie. Even on a cold, snowy, windy day, he is excited to fetch sticks! I bundle up from head to toe, and off we go. It always feels good to get home where I sit next to the fire and warm up with a cup of hot tea. Enjoy the snow!

—Beth